I0784060

Silver Light

AND THE RED CANYON

By Nan C. Cataldi

Illustrated by
Thomas Rodriguez

INKWELL BOOKS
Writing-Publishing-Printing

ISBN 978-1-7366445-4-6

Library of Congress Control Number: 2021231862

Published by Inkwell Books LLC

10632 North Scottsdale Road, Unit 695

Scottsdale, AZ 85254

Tel. 480-315-3781

E-mail info@inkwellbooksllc.com

Website www.inkwellbooksllc.com

Dedication

This book was inspired by my 4-year-old granddaughter, Selena, for her incredible imagination and love of animals.

Many years ago, in the mountains of the southwest, lived an unusual horse. He was found as a baby by a herd of wild horses one moonlit night.

He had a special silver-white coat and shiny,
silver mane which shimmered in the moonlight,
so they called him Silver Light.

2

In no time he grew into a handsome stallion,
larger than the other horses.

Because he looked different, the black, brown, and
pinto horses of his herd began to ignore him.
So, he began spending most days alone,
grazing far from the main herd.

4

One day Silver Light decided to leave the herd.
He wanted to find other horses that looked like him.

5

The stallion's journey took him to a nearby canyon with red colored mountains and beautiful waterfalls.

He was very thirsty when he arrived, so he headed toward the large stream in the center of the canyon.

While he was drinking, a gray hawk swooped down from a nearby tree and landed next to him.

"Wow! I have never seen a horse like you before,
except on the Great Red Rock."

The silver horse looked up at the hawk. "Oh, no! I was hoping to find more horses that looked like me here."

10

"I have flown over all the canyon," the hawk said.
"No horses like you live here anymore.
You may be the only one left."

The beautiful horse lowered his head.
He was so sad. "But my herd does not accept me.
That is why I came here. I am so lonely."

"You can stay here with all of us," the hawk said.
"I know all the animals here will welcome you.
The writings on the rock say horses like you
come from the spirits above.

The animals in our canyon tell of a spirit horse who came here in ancient times. You are very special! Come with me, and I will show you."

The hawk guided the horse to a huge red rock
at the entrance of a cave. It showed pictures of
a white horse with wings.

"The animals tell of a spirit horse, who was sent from the sky to help the canyon animals and birds when there was a great drought. The river was drying up. All the plants and trees began to wilt, and their green leaves turned brown.

Early one moonlit night, a bright ball of silver light
appeared in the sky over the canyon.

An owl, a coyote, a pair of raccoons, a squirrel, a fox, and even a mountain lion followed it to the side of a tall mountain next to the dried-up stream.

"When the light winked out, a beautiful, silver-white, winged horse appeared. The writing on the rock says she was magical.

She landed on a ledge in the middle of a tall red mountain. Then stomped her right hoof twice.

20

Water began to flow like a waterfall
to the dry stream below.

The animals that had gathered there, rejoiced as water filled the dry stream. This magical horse lived here for one hundred years, helping the canyon plants and animals to thrive.

Then, one night when the moon was full, she spread her massive wings and flew back into the sky.

23

They say sometimes on a summer night you can see her in the stars above. She must be your ancestor."

The horse smiled. "Thank you for the story.
I will stay here and make the canyon my home."

Silver Light lived happily with all the living creatures
in the canyon for almost thirty years, helping them.

One moonlit night, a bright, silver ball of light appeared in the sky and lit up the canyon. The ball transformed into a magnificent, silver-white winged, spirit horse.

27

She landed next to Silver Light. Then she spoke softly
to the old horse, "It is time you come home with me."

28

The spirit horse stomped her hooves and shining magic began to spin around the old horse. Wings suddenly appeared on the stallion's shoulders.

Then Silver Light, too, turned into a spirit horse, spread his new wings, and the two horses flew into the sky.

30

The hawk and many of the other canyon animals gathered to watch as the spirits flew higher and higher into the sky, until both horses disappeared.

Within seconds two bright stars appeared in the sky over the canyon. Silver Light was finally home.

About the Author

Nan C. Cataldi was born and raised in a small town in western Pennsylvania. After raising her two children in Richmond, Virginia, she decided to move out to the Old West. She is now retired from the medical professional and currently resides in western Pennsylvania. How-
ever, she lived in Arizona for many years, which influenced several of her books. Nan has taken children's story writing classes over the years and written many short stories. Since she was young, she has had a talent for story-telling and a great imagination. In addition to the "Keys of Being" trilogy, she also writes picture books.

About the Illustrator

Tom Rodriguez has spent his 30-year career as an illustrator and graphic designer. He is owner of TJR Designs in Phoenix, Arizona. Tom has illustrated several books, and hundreds of book covers over the course of his career. He also specializes in logo and advertising design, and frequently creates branding materials that range from brochures to large signage.

Creating the artwork for Nancy Cataldi's wonderful story of Silver Light was a truly rewarding experience for Tom. He would like to thank Nancy for this incredible opportunity.

Tom may be reached through his website www.tjrdesigns.com.